Dear Parent:
Your child's love of reading starts here!

Every child learns to read in a different way and at his or her own speed. Some go back and forth between reading levels and read favorite books again and again. Others read through each level in order. You can help your young reader improve and become more confident by encouraging his or her own interests and abilities. From books your child reads with you to the first books he or she reads alone, there are I Can Read Books for every stage of reading:

SHARED READING
Basic language, word repetition, and whimsical illustrations, ideal for sharing with your emerg

D0840045

BEGINNING READING
Short sentences, familiar words, a
for children eager to read on their own

READING WITH HELP
Engaging stories, longer sentences, and language play
for developing readers

READING ALONE
Complex plots, challenging vocabulary, and high-interest topics
for the independent reader

I Can Read Books have introduced children to the joy of reading since 1957. Featuring award-winning authors and illustrators and a fabulous cast of beloved characters, I Can Read Books set the standard for beginning readers.

A lifetime of discovery begins with the magical words **"I Can Read!"**

Visit www.icanread.com for information
on enriching your child's reading experience.

Clarion Books is an imprint of HarperCollins Publishers.
I Can Read® and I Can Read Book® are trademarks of HarperCollins Publishers.
Pretzel and the Puppies: Meet the Pups!
Copyright © 2022 by HarperCollins Publishers LLC
All rights reserved. Printed in the United States of America. No part of this book may be used
or reproduced in any manner whatsoever without written permission except in the case of brief
quotations embodied in critical articles and reviews. For information address HarperCollins Children's
Books, a division of HarperCollins Publishers, 195 Broadway, New York, NY 10007.
www.icanread.com

ISBN 978-0-35-868360-5 HC
ISBN 978-0-35-868361-2 PA

Typography by Stephanie Hays
22 23 24 25 26 LB   10 9 8 7 6 5 4 3 2 1   First Edition

I Can Read!

BEGINNING 1 READING

PRETZEL AND THE PUPPIES

MEET THE PUPS!

Margret and H. A. Rey

CLARION BOOKS
An Imprint of HarperCollins *Publishers*

This is Pretzel.

He is a very long dog.

And these are his puppies:

Puck, Pippa, Pedro, Paxton, and Poppy.

They play games and solve problems.

They have a lot of fun together!

This is Greta.

She is the pups' mom.

She is also the mayor of Muttgomery.

Muttgomery is a city of dogs!

6

Puck, Paxton, Pedro, Pippa, and Poppy
make a great team.

Paxton is an artist.

He loves to draw and paint.

When he sees something beautiful

he has to draw it!

Poppy is a leader.

She reads a lot of books.

She is full of great ideas.

Nothing stops her!

Puck is funny.

He tells great jokes.

He likes to make his family laugh.

Dogs always smile when he is around.

Pippa is a performer.

She is a singer and a dancer.

She loves to get dressed up.

Fancy is fun!

Pedro is an athlete.

He may be small, but he is strong!

He loves to fetch and run.

He never gives up.

The pups love their city.

They love to help their neighbors.

Living in Muttgomery is the best!

They want to celebrate Muttgomery
with their friends.

But how? They need a plan.

Time to get your paws up, pups!

21

The pups decide to have a parade.

They gather all they need.

Pedro will ride his scooter.

Paxton and Poppy use art supplies

to make decorations.

Pippa and Puck find costumes.

The pups are ready!

The puppy parade is off!

But a parade needs lots of dogs.

How will the pups make their parade

big enough to celebrate Muttgomery?

The pups can solve this problem.

Get your paws up, pups!

They spread the word.

Every dog in town will join in!

The dogs of Muttgomery

make a long parade.

They walk, roll, and sing songs.

They have fun being together.

Great job, pups.

You made a difference today.

You made your bark!